For Aphra O'Brien
with lots of love

Special thanks to
Sue Mongredien

ORCHARD BOOKS
338 Euston Road, London NW1 3BH
Orchard Books Australia
Level 17/207 Kent Street, Sydney, NSW 2000
A Paperback Original

First published in 2008 by Orchard Books.

HiT entertainment

A CIP catalogue record for this book is available
from the British Library.

ISBN 978 1 84616 888 8
10

Printed in Great Britain

Orchard Books is a division of Hachette Children's Books,
an Hachette UK company

www.hachette.co.uk

Helena
the Horseriding
Fairy

by Daisy Meadows

ORCHARD

The
Fairyland
Palace

Fairyla

Car Park

Coaches

Riding Stables

Cooke Football
Stadium

Netball Courts

Football
Pitches

Tippington
Town

LEISURE CENTRE

Swimming Pool

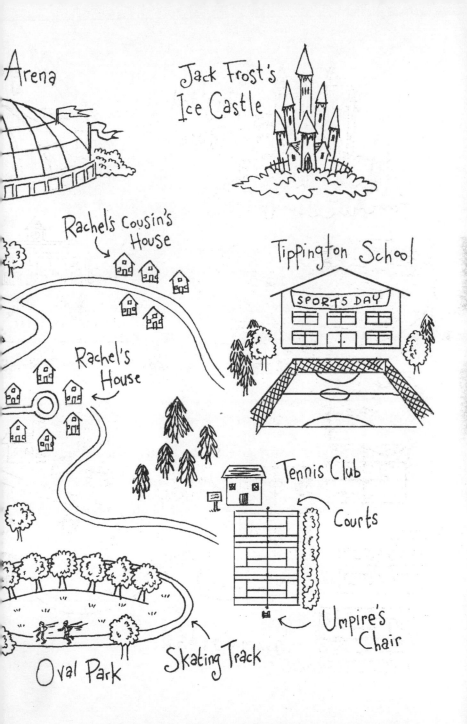

Arena

Jack Frost's
Ice Castle

Rachel's Cousin's
House

Tippington School

SPORTS DAY

Rachel's
House

Tennis Club

Courts

Umpire's
Chair

Oval Park

Skating Track

The Fairyland Olympics are about to start,
And my crafty goblins are going to take part.
We'll win this year, for I've got a cunning plan.
I'm sending my goblins to the arena in Fairyland.

The Magic Sporty Objects that make sports safe and fun,
Will be stolen by my goblins, to keep until we've won.
Sporty Fairies, prepare to lose and to watch us win.
Goblins, follow my commands, and let the games begin!

Contents

Magic Message

"There," Rachel Walker said, tidying her hair. "I'm ready. Are you?"

Kirsty Tate buttoned her jodhpurs and smiled at her best friend. "Yes," she said. "I can't wait!"

It was the first day of the Easter holidays, and Kirsty had come to stay with Rachel's family for a week.

In a few minutes, they would be setting
off for a riding lesson at the Tippington
Stables, and both girls were looking
forward to it. They always seemed
to have the best fun when they
were together – and the most
exciting adventures.

Kirsty was just about to open the door,
when something caught her eye. The
pages of Rachel's diary were fluttering
as it lay on her bed, and yet there was
no breeze in the room. "Rachel!" she
said, pointing. "Look!"

She and Rachel ran over excitedly. They had each been given matching bejewelled diaries by the King and Queen of Fairyland, as thank-you presents for helping the fairies. The two girls had been friends with the fairies long enough now to know that the fluttering pages of the book meant only one thing: something magical was about to happen!

Kirsty held her breath as the diary fell open at two blank pages, and then she gasped as sparkly gold writing appeared on the paper, letter by letter.

"It's a message," Rachel whispered, her heart pounding.

We…need…your…help! the golden letters spelled.

11

We
need
your
help...

"The fairies must be in trouble!"
Kirsty cried. "Do you think Jack Frost
has been up to more mischief?"

"There's only one way to find out,"
Rachel said, and Kirsty nodded.

Both girls opened the golden lockets
around their necks, and took out pinches
of fairy dust.

"Let's go to Fairyland," said Kirsty,
flinging the fairy dust over herself.

"To Fairyland!" Rachel echoed, doing the same, and the two girls were immediately swept up in a magical whirlwind of rainbow-coloured sparkles. As they were whisked along, they felt themselves shrinking to become fairies. Kirsty smiled as she glanced over her shoulder and saw a pair of delicate, gossamer wings on her back, glittering with magic.

Helena

Seconds later, they were set down
gently in Fairyland, in front of
an unfamiliar building.
It was very grand, with
white marble walls
and glittering golden
pillars at the front.
King Oberon
and Queen
Titania stepped
forward to greet
the girls, with seven
other fairies that
Rachel and Kirsty
didn't recognise.

"Thank you for
coming," the King said.

"Yes, thank you," the Queen
added. "We called you because our

Sporty Fairies really need your help." She gestured to the fairies who stood nearby and introduced them. "This is Helena the Horseriding Fairy, Francesca the Football Fairy, Zoe the Skating Fairy, Naomi the Netball Fairy, Samantha the Swimming Fairy, Alice the Tennis Fairy and Gemma the Gymnastics Fairy." Each fairy smiled and said hello, looking pleased to see Rachel and Kirsty.

"Hello," Rachel said, curtseying to the King and Queen and smiling at the Sporty Fairies. Then she looked around curiously. "Um… Where are we? I don't recognise this part of Fairyland."

"This is the Fairyland Arena," Helena explained, "where all the sporting events take place."

"Come and see," the Queen said, waving at the golden doors. They swung open immediately, and Kirsty and Rachel followed the fairies through to a large stadium. There were rows of white seats surrounding a football pitch of the greenest grass the girls had ever seen.

"Wow," Kirsty breathed. "My dad would love this!"

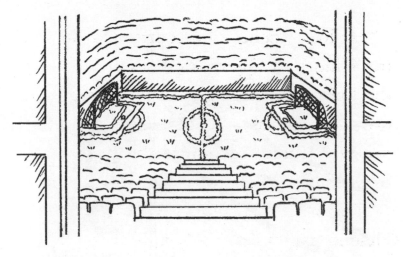

"That's not all," Samantha told them. "If we need to change it for a different sport, we just do this…" She waved her wand and a stream of sparkly fairy dust billowed out. The football pitch gleamed a bright gold, and a rainbow-coloured mist descended upon it. Then the mist cleared, and, where the grass had been seconds before, there was now a swimming pool, its turquoise water shimmering in the sunshine.

Rachel blinked. "That's amazing!" she marvelled.

The Queen smiled. "Our Sporty Fairies help make sports fun and exciting, both in Fairyland and in the human world," she explained.

"And we also make sure sporting events run smoothly, and that everyone plays fairly," added Zoe.

"How do you manage that?"
Kirsty asked.

"With our Magic Sporty Objects,"
Francesca told her. "I have a Magic
Football, Gemma has a Magic Hoop,
Alice has a Magic Tennis Racquet..."

"Not any more, though," Alice chipped
in sadly. "Because our Magic Sporty
Objects have been stolen!"

Burglars
Break In

"Stolen?" echoed Kirsty. "What happened?"

"Well," Naomi began, "when we're not using our magic objects, we keep them in our lockers here at the arena. But when we came to collect them this morning, the lockers were empty!"

"So who could have taken them?" Rachel asked. Then she sighed.

She already knew the answer.

Gemma nodded, as if reading Rachel's mind. "Yes," she said. "Jack Frost and his goblins. We have special keys that open our lockers," – she showed the girls a tiny key, shaped like a bow, that she wore on a silver chain around her neck – "and we think Jack Frost used his special ice magic to forge copies of them."

"Then he sent his goblins to break into our lockers and steal our magic objects," Zoe went on.

"Let's go to the seeing pool," Queen Titania suggested. "Then we can watch how it happened." She waved her wand and they were all whisked up in a sparkly magic whirlwind which took them to the edge of a clear blue pool in the palace gardens. The queen waved her wand once more, and the pool rippled with colour.

The girls watched as images appeared on the water. There were the seven Sporty Fairies flying towards the arena at dawn, the sun streaking the sky orange and red. Down below were

23

several goblins: one stumbling as he
kicked a football, two others trying
to throw a netball to each other, but
missing every time, and others falling
over as they practised handstands and
cartwheels. Kirsty and Rachel watched
as the Sporty Fairies flew down towards
the goblins.

"We always try to help anyone if they're struggling at sport," Francesca explained.

"But it was all a trick," Gemma sighed. "The goblins were just trying to distract us, and keep us away from the locker room!"

The water in the pool rippled and the image changed again. Now Rachel and Kirsty could see seven goblins, dressed in black with balaclavas on their heads, climbing a rope up a wall towards an open window in the arena. They kept slipping and treading on each other but, eventually, they all scrambled in through the window.

"That's the window of the locker room," Samantha told the girls. "*Our* locker room!"

Once inside, the tallest goblin shouted, "Ice keys at the ready!" and each goblin took an icy key from his pocket  and tried it in the locker before him.

There was chaos at first, as the goblins couldn't find the right doors for their keys, but eventually they got there. As the last key went in, all seven doors sprang open, revealing the Magic Sporty Objects inside: a hard hat, a football, a skate lace, a netball, goggles, a tennis racquet and a hoop – all sparkling with fairy magic.

Each goblin grabbed one of the Magic Sporty Objects eagerly.

"Now, remember what Jack Frost told us," the tallest goblin said. "If we're going to win the Fairyland Olympics, we need to practise our sports with the other goblins. But make sure you keep the magic objects well hidden in the human world while you practise so the fairies can't find them! Then, in a week, we'll come back to Fairyland...and win the Olympics!"

The other goblins cheered and then
they all sprinted back to the window.
Rachel couldn't help noticing how much
more athletic they
seemed now that they
had the Magic
Sporty Objects.
The goblin with
the hoop even
did a series of
backflips across the floor!

Then the scene in the pool faded,
and the water became clear again.

"The Fairyland Olympics start in seven
days," King Oberon explained, "and
Jack Frost knows that when the Magic
Sporty Objects are away from the Sporty
Fairies, or their lockers, sporting events
will be ruined everywhere, because

nobody will be able to enjoy sports as usual."

The Queen nodded. "He also knows that the Magic Sporty Objects are so powerful that they make anyone near them perform very well at sport," she added. "He wants his goblins to win the Olympics, so he can get his hands on the prize."

"What is the prize?" Kirsty asked.

"The Fairyland Olympics Cup," the Queen replied. "It's filled with luck — which would mean Jack Frost could get away with all sorts of new mischief!"

"Can the Olympics be cancelled until the Magic Sporty Objects are found?" Rachel suggested.

"No," the King sighed. "The Fairyland Olympics

are linked to the human Olympics. If we cancel our event, it would cause great disruption to the ones in your world."

"That's right," Zoe said. "But while we don't have our magical objects, nobody will be able to play well."

"Nobody will be enjoying sport very much either," Francesca added.

"We've just got to get our objects back," Naomi cried. "Otherwise both Olympic Games, and all sports, will be ruined!"

Girls on the Case

"We'll help you in any way we can," Rachel said at once.

"Thank you," Helena replied. "We know the goblins will be practising their new skills, so it's likely they'll turn up in places connected with each object."

"We're going riding today," Kirsty remembered. "Maybe the goblin with

your Magic Hard Hat will be there,
Helena." In her green riding jacket,
cream jodhpurs and boots, Kirsty
thought Helena was dressed perfectly
for riding, except that she was missing

the special hard hat
that all riders need.
Helena looked
excited. "I'll
come with you
in case he is,"
she said. "Let's
go back to your
world straight away!"

The girls just had time to say
goodbye to the fairies before Helena
waved her wand and whisked them
back to Rachel's room, turning the girls
back to their normal sizes once more.

"Are you ready, girls?" they heard
Mr Walker calling.

Helena tucked herself into Kirsty's
pocket and the girls hurried downstairs.
Rachel's dad was waiting to drive them
to the stables. Both girls felt tingly with
excitement as they got into the car; it
was wonderful to be starting a new
fairy adventure!

It was only a short ride to Tippington
Stables and soon Mr Walker was
parking the car.

"Have fun," he told the girls as they
jumped out. "I'll come and pick you up
at the end of your lesson."

"Bye, Dad!" Rachel called. She
turned to Kirsty. "Our instructor is
called Vivian," she said. "Let's go and
find her."

As the girls walked
towards the stables,
Helena peeked out
of Kirsty's pocket.
"I can sense a lot
of disruption here,"
she said anxiously.
"I wonder what's going on."

Rachel and Kirsty walked in through
the stable yard entrance and then
stopped in horror at the chaos that
greeted them. Horses and ponies were
trotting to and fro without riders while
the stable hands ran around trying to
catch them. One girl was trying to
mount, but the girth on her pony
hadn't been done up tightly enough so
the saddle immediately slipped, tipping
the rider straight off onto the ground.

Kirsty helped the girl to her feet. Luckily she was unhurt and thanked Kirsty before going back to her horse.

A lady with red hair bustled over, and Helena ducked down into Kirsty's pocket again.

"Hello, Vivian," Rachel said to the red-haired lady. "Is everything... all right?"

Vivian sighed. "I'm afraid it's rather
hectic today, girls!" she said, "but I'm
trying to sort everything out
before your lesson.
You're on Shadow,
Rachel, and your
friend, Kirsty, will
be on Brandy. Why
don't you go and
tack up? I'll be
with you as soon as
I've got everything
under control."

"OK," Rachel said,
as she and Kirsty set off
to find their ponies.
They'd hardly taken a step when a
rider went careering past – sitting the
wrong way round on her pony.

"Oh, no!" Vivian cried, rushing to help. "I'll meet you in the paddock, girls!" she called over her shoulder.

Helena peeked out again. "This is awful," she said despairingly. "And it's all because my Magic Hard Hat is missing. If I had that, then none of this would be happening!" Suddenly she frowned as if she was deep in concentration. Then her tiny face brightened. "It's here," she said in her clear silvery voice. "My Magic Hard Hat is here — I can sense it." She stared in dismay as another horse trotted past without a rider on its back. "But we've got to find it soon," she added, "before things get any worse!"

A Sweet Idea

Rachel and Kirsty went to tack up,
keeping an eye out for any goblins that
might have Helena's Magic Hard Hat.

"Good boy, Brandy," Kirsty said,
patting her toffee-coloured pony as she
adjusted her stirrups. Brandy tossed his
head impatiently as Kirsty attempted
to get the stirrups even, but one of

the stirrup leathers just wouldn't go any shorter.

"Ah!" said Helena, flying on to Kirsty's shoulder. "It's because my hat is missing that you're having so much trouble, but I know a trick that might help. If you twist the strap around the stirrup, it'll make it a little shorter. Watch!" She waved her wand and Kirsty watched in delight as the stirrup leather came undone, looped itself through the stirrup and then did itself up again, making the stirrups perfectly even.

44

"Thank you, Helena," Kirsty smiled.

Meanwhile, Rachel was having trouble getting Shadow to take the bit in his mouth.

"Everything's more difficult because my hat's missing," Helena sighed. "Let me try, Rachel." She hovered close to Shadow's left ear and spoke gently to him. Rachel couldn't hear what she said, but Shadow was suddenly happy to take the bit.

"Thanks," Rachel said gratefully. "Vivian said we should meet her in the paddock, didn't she? Let's head over there now."

The girls led their ponies through the
stable yard and out to the paddock,
but, when they arrived, they were
surprised to see a boy already there
on a grey horse. He was cantering
in a circle, riding confidently and with
skill – he was certainly having much
more success than anyone else they'd
seen that day.

The girls stopped and watched closely.
As the grey horse
jumped over a brush
box, the boy's hard
hat lifted up ever
so slightly. Kirsty
gasped; the
movement of the
boy's hat had just
revealed a pointy
green nose!

"He's a goblin!" she whispered to
Rachel and Helena.

"And he's wearing my hat!" Helena
exclaimed crossly.

Rachel frowned. "But it's so big,"
she said. "The hat, I mean. I was
expecting it to be the same size as
it was in Fairyland."

"No," Helena said. "You see, the Magic Sporty Objects adjust their size to suit whoever is holding them."

"So how are we going to get it back?" Kirsty wondered. "If the goblin sees us coming after his hat, he'll just ride away."

Rachel thought hard. "Helena, what do horses like to eat more than anything else?" she asked.

"Most horses love sugar lumps," the little fairy replied. "Why?"

Rachel smiled. "Could you use your magic to conjure some up?" she asked.

Helena nodded. "Of course," she said, waving her wand.

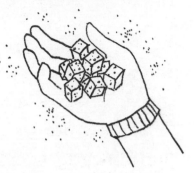

Immediately,
a pile of sparkling
white sugar cubes
appeared in
Rachel's hand.

"Great!" Rachel declared. "Now, how about we try tempting that horse over to us with a trail of sugar lumps? Then we might be able to persuade the goblin to give us back the hat!"

"Good idea," said Kirsty.

Helena waved her wand again, and a flurry of horseshoe-shaped fairy dust swirled all around the pile of sugar lumps. Then, one by one, the cubes jumped down from Rachel's hand and started bouncing along the grass, lining up to make a trail from the girls towards the horse.

It didn't take long for the grey horse to spot the sugar lumps. She had been cantering but she slowed at the sight of her favourite snack, and immediately dipped her head to eat one of the sugar lumps.

The goblin seemed a little confused at the appearance of the sugar, and he looked around. Then he noticed the girls in the corner of the paddock, and frowned. "What are you doing here?"

he asked. Then a suspicious look came over his face and he touched the hat protectively. "Hey – you haven't seen any fairies around here, have you?"

Rachel and Kirsty exchanged glances and gulped. How were they going to answer that question truthfully without scaring the goblin away?

A Ride to the Rescue

Rachel thought quickly. "Fairies? I can't see any fairies," she replied, and it was quite true — since Helena was now hiding at the bottom of Kirsty's pocket.

"That hat you're wearing..." Kirsty said to the goblin as the grey horse came nearer, eating the next sugar lump in the line. "It's not yours, is it?"

The goblin gave a crafty smile. "No, but I'm keeping it," he told her, and winked. "This hat is going to help my team win at the Fairyland Olympics!"

"But that would be cheating," Rachel said. "Listen… If you give it back to us, we can return it to its rightful owner."

The goblin cackled and shook his head. "Not likely," he said. "It's mine now. Oh, I'll show those fairies a thing or – Hey!" He broke off in surprise as

Helena shot out of Kirsty's pocket and zoomed towards him, a determined look on her face. "Oi! What are you doing?" the goblin cried as she flew towards the hat. She pushed at it with her tiny hands, but, unfortunately, she was too small and she couldn't move it one bit.

"Oh, no, you don't!" the goblin yelled. He butted Helena away, tugged on his horse's reins, and cantered off, leaving the fairy fluttering in his wake.

"You can't catch
me!" he yelled
gleefully over
his shoulder.

Rachel and
Kirsty ran over
to their own
ponies, mounted
them quickly and
urged them to chase
after the goblin. Helena
flew alongside. "Try to stay as close to
the goblin as you can," she encouraged
them. "While you're near my Magic
Hard Hat, its power will affect you, too,
so you'll be able to ride well."

"OK," Kirsty replied, hunching
lower over Brandy and urging him
to go faster.

"But it works both ways," Helena
added. "The further you are from
the hat, the worse your riding
will become."

"Come on, Shadow," Rachel urged.
"Keep going!"

The girls gradually gained ground
on the goblin and soon realised that
Helena was right. The nearer they
got to him, the easier it was to ride.

But then the goblin glanced over his shoulder and looked panicked to see how close the girls were getting. He urged his horse on and it broke into a gallop, pulling away from Brandy and Shadow.

As the gap widened, Kirsty could feel her control slipping. Brandy stumbled on a tufty bit of grass, and slowed nervously.

Rachel, too, was struggling to stay
in her saddle, but she knew they had
to get closer to the goblin's horse again.
"Come on, boy," she said
encouragingly. "You can do it!"

All three of them were now
approaching a tall hedge that bordered
the paddock. It was a huge jump, but
the goblin's horse didn't
hesitate and took it
at full speed.
Thanks to the
magic of the
hard hat, the
horse cleared
the hedge
easily, leaving
the girls behind
on the other side.

With the tall hedge now between them, the effect of the Magic Hard Hat wore off completely, and Rachel bumped horribly on Shadow's back.

Kirsty, too, was being jolted around, and felt very frightened. She was getting closer and closer to the hedge, which looked more enormous by the second. She wasn't at all confident that Brandy was going to be able to jump high enough, not when her riding skills seemed to have vanished. She tried frantically to think of a way to stop her pony, but her mind was blank with fright. She couldn't remember what to do!

Kirsty glanced over at Rachel, wondering if her friend could help, but Rachel looked just as terrified. She was white-faced, clinging on to Shadow for dear life as he thundered towards the hedge.

Kirsty's hands were sweating, and suddenly the reins slipped from her grasp altogether. "Help!" she cried, as she felt herself falling...

Helena Helps

Just as Kirsty thought she was about to hit the ground, there was a flash of bright pink light in her eyes, and she felt herself shrinking. Down, down, down she went, smaller and smaller, until she was a fairy with shining fairy wings. She fluttered her wings thankfully and soared into the air.

Rachel was doing
the same, and
both girls flew
gratefully over
to Helena.
"Thank you,"
gasped Rachel.
"That was scary!"

Brandy and Shadow both jumped
over the hedge without their riders, and
then came to a stop in the next field,
putting their heads down to graze.

Seeing that their ponies
were safe, the three
fairies zoomed after
the goblin, whose
horse was still
galloping.

"We've got to think
of a way to get that
hat off his head," Rachel
said as they flew. "But how?"

"Helena, could your magic undo
the strap?" Kirsty wondered. Helena
nodded, and Kirsty pointed towards
a jump the goblin's horse was now
approaching. "If we can catch up with
him in time, maybe you could magic
the buckle undone just after the jump,"
she said. "Then, as his horse lands,
the hat should fly off his head…"

"And we can catch it!" Rachel finished.

"Brilliant idea," Helena said warmly. "Let's do it!"

The three fairies flew on towards the goblin. "Of course, once the hat comes off his head, he won't be able to ride very well any more," Helena murmured to herself, "so I'll have to make sure he's all right."

"He's coming up to the jump!" Rachel cried.

Helena pointed her wand at the Magic Hard Hat. As the goblin's horse rose up to meet the fence, a swirling cloud of pink fairy dust fluttered in the air. As the goblin landed on the other side, the strap slid smoothly through the buckle and came undone – and the hat lifted, too, straight off the goblin's head!

As the hat flew through the air, Rachel and Kirsty darted towards it and caught it between them. Immediately, the hat shimmered and then shrank down to its Fairyland size.

Meanwhile, the goblin had completely lost control of his horse and had bounced right out of the saddle.

"Whoaaaa!" he cried in alarm as he tumbled towards the ground.

But Helena deftly flicked her wand at a nearby water trough, which whizzed

through the air and stopped just under the tumbling goblin. He fell into the water with a mighty *splash!* Kirsty and Rachel couldn't help chuckling. They knew goblins hated getting wet. "It serves him right, for trying to cheat," Rachel said, as the goblin clambered out of the trough, dripping wet.

"Maybe you should go back to Fairyland and dry off!" Helena called as he stomped off in a huff.

Kirsty and Rachel gave the Magic Hard Hat to Helena, who popped it back on her head with a smile of relief.

"Thank you," she said, and touched her wand to it. There was a flash of twinkling pink lights all around the hat.

"There," she said happily. "I've just set everything to rights. Horseriding is a lot more safe and fun again for everyone!"

"Hurrah!" cheered Rachel and Kirsty.

Helena gave them both a hug, then waved her wand to turn them back to their normal sizes. "Thanks again, girls," she said. "I'll fly to Fairyland now and tell the others the good news!"

"Bye, Helena,"
Kirsty said,
waving as she
and Rachel
watched the little
fairy zoom away.

"Oh, girls, there you are! And you've
found Mischief, well done!" came
a voice, and Vivian strode into
the paddock.

Rachel and Kirsty looked at each other, realising that Mischief must be the name of the grey horse the goblin had been riding. "Yes, she was in the paddock," Rachel said truthfully. "We followed her here."

Vivian looked very relieved. "Thank goodness," she said. "She must have got loose in all the turmoil. Thank you, girls. I'll take her back to the stables, then we can begin your lesson. I'm sorry for the slow start today, but everything seems to be back to normal in the yard now."

Kirsty and Rachel smiled at each other. They knew why everything was

back to normal. It was because Helena
the Horseriding Fairy had her Magic
Hard Hat back again.

"That was exciting," Rachel said,
as she mounted Shadow, noticing
how much easier it was this time.

Kirsty nodded. "Yes," she said. "Now we just have to find the other six Magic Sporty Objects in time for the Fairyland Olympics." She grinned. "I think this is going to be a *fairy* busy week!"

Now Rachel and Kirsty
must help...

Francesca the Football Fairy

Read on for a sneak peek...

"You look great, Dad!" Rachel Walker laughed, glancing at her father as she climbed out of the car. Mr Walker was wearing a blue and white football shirt and scarf, his face was painted with blue and white stripes, and he had a fluffy blue and white wig on his head.

"The wig's fantastic!" Kirsty Tate, Rachel's best friend, added with a grin. She was staying with the Walkers over the spring holiday. "He's going to be the best-dressed Tippington Rovers supporter here."

Rachel nodded. "I'm glad Mum and I are just wearing scarves, though," she added. "That wig looks a bit hot!"

"It is, but I want to show my support for the team," said Mr Walker, as they left the car park and joined the other football fans heading towards the Cooke Stadium. "This is a very important match, girls. If Tippington beat Alton United today, the team will be promoted to the next league!"

Rachel and Kirsty exchanged concerned glances.

They were both worried that the football match would be a complete disaster, because the Sporty Fairies had lost their Magic Sporty Objects. When these special objects were in their proper places, with the Sporty Fairies or in the fairies' lockers, they made sure that sport in both the human and fairy worlds was safe, fun and exciting. Unfortunately, they'd been stolen by cunning Jack Frost and his goblin servants...

Read Francesca the Football Fairy to find out what adventures are in store for Kirsty and Rachel!

Meet the
Sporty Fairies

Join Rachel and Kirsty as they help the Sporty Fairies
foil Jack Frost's naughty plot to mess up
the Fairyland Olympics!

www.rainbowmagicbooks.co.uk

Meet the fairies, play games
and get sneak peeks at
the latest books!

www.rainbowmagicbooks.co.uk

There's fairy fun for everyone on
our wonderful website.
You'll find great activities, competitions, stories and
fairy profiles, and also a special newsletter.

Get 30% off all Rainbow Magic books at

www.rainbowmagicbooks.co.uk

Enter the code RAINBOW at the checkout.
Offer ends 31 December 2012.

Offer valid in United Kingdom and Republic of Ireland only.

Win Rainbow Magic Goodies!

There are lots of Rainbow Magic fairies, and we want to know which one is your favourite! Send us a picture of her and tell us in thirty words why she is your favourite and why you like Rainbow Magic books. Each month we will put the entries into a draw and select one winner to receive a Rainbow Magic Sparkly T-shirt and Goody Bag!

Send your entry on a postcard to Rainbow Magic Competition, Orchard Books, 338 Euston Road, London NW1 3BH. Australian readers should email: childrens.books@hachette.com.au New Zealand readers should write to Rainbow Magic Competition, 4 Whetu Place, Mairangi Bay, Auckland NZ. Don't forget to include your name and address. Only one entry per child.

Good luck!

Meet the
Music Fairies

Join Kirsty and Rachel as they outwit the naughty
goblins to get back the Music Fairies'
stolen instruments!

www.rainbowmagicbooks.co.uk